This book belongs to

_____

_____

For Oliver Churchill Fuge
born 2 December, 2004
C.F.

This edition published by Parragon Books Ltd in 2017 and distributed by

Parragon Inc.
440 Park Avenue South, 13th Floor
New York, NY 10016
www.parragon.com

Text and illustrations by © Charles Fuge 2005

ISBN 978-1-5270-0920-2

Printed in China

Swim, Little Wombat, SWIM!

Written and illustrated by

Charles Fuge

PaRragon

Bath · New York · Cologne · Melbourne · Delhi
Hong Kong · Shenzhen · Singapore

Little Wombat was looking for apples.
"Hello," said a squeaky voice he didn't recognize.
Little Wombat spun around.
"Hello! I'm Wombat," he said. "Who are you?"
"I'm Platypus," said the stranger.

Then, Platypus
waddled over to the
pond and disappeared
under the water.

"PLA-TY-PUS!" Little Wombat
giggled. "PLA-TY-PUS!"

He tried to waddle, too. He giggled
and waddled, closer and closer to the
water's edge . . .

Little Wombat sank like a stone.

In a flash, Platypus
darted towards him.

Before he knew it, Wombat
was at the surface . . .

. . . and safely out of the water.
"Thank you, Platypus," he spluttered.
"How did you learn to swim like that?"
"It's easy!" Platypus smiled.
"I'll teach you!"

First, Little Wombat had to hold
on to the edge and kick his legs
as hard as he could.

Then, he splashed all around the pond.

He splashed and kicked until
he was worn out.
"Time for lunch!" said Platypus.

Little Wombat munched on juicy, red apples and Platypus munched on a handful of shrimp.

"Never swim on a full tummy," said Platypus. So they snoozed in the shade for an hour.

That afternoon, Little Wombat
learned to paddle with his arms . . .

. . . and dive like a frog!

Then, through all the splashing,
Little Wombat heard his
name being called.

Rabbit and Koala had come to see
what he had been doing all day.
Little Wombat beamed.
"PLATYPUS taught me to swim," he said.
"Come on, Platypus, let's race."

WOM-BA-AT, WOM-BA-AT!"

Koala and Rabbit
cheered him on.

"No . . . not Wombat . . ."
Little Wombat said and
grinned at his new friend.

"WOM-BATYPUS!"